The Adventures of Pinocchio

TREASURY OF ILLUSTRATED CLASSICS™

The Adventures of Pinocchio

by
Carlo Collodi

Adapted by
Kathleen Rizzi

Illustrated by
Bob Berry

Kappa Books Publishers, LLC.

Cover art by Julia Lundman

Contents

CHAPTER 1

An Unusual Piece of Wood

Once there was a piece of wood that was unlike any other. At first, it didn't seem different from any piece of wood that you would use to burn in wintertime stoves or fireplaces.

Mister Antonio, who was called Mister Cherry because of the bright red tip of his nose, chose that piece of wood to make a new leg for his table. He soon learned just how different a piece of wood it was.

With his ax held high overhead, Mister Cherry was just about to hit the log when he heard a voice. "Please don't

hit me too hard," it begged.

Mister Cherry looked around the room. No one was there. He looked under the workbench and in the cupboard. No one was there. He looked in a basket of wood shavings and sawdust. Still he found no one. He even opened the door to the shop and looked up and down the street. No one was there.

"Oh, I must be imagining things," he said as he raised the ax again. When he brought the ax down, it hit the wood just where he wished, splitting the log.

"That hurt!" cried the same voice from before. Mister Cherry was suddenly afraid. His jaw hung wide open, and his tongue stuck out of his mouth.

"Is it possible that this piece of wood can speak and feel and cry like a child?" he wondered. "I don't believe it. Perhaps someone is inside the wood. If there is, I'll teach him a lesson!"

Mister Cherry struck the wood against the walls and waited to see if the voice spoke again. It didn't, so he picked up the plane to begin to shape the wood to make the table leg. As he slid the plane over the piece of wood, it began to jiggle and wiggle in his hands.

"Stop, stop, you're tickling me!" the wood laughed.

Mister Cherry fell to the floor in shock. When at last he sat up again, his face—even his red nose—was blue with fright.

It was a very unusual piece of wood

indeed!

Before Mister Cherry could think of what to do, there was a knock at the door. "Come in," he called from where he was sitting on the floor.

Geppetto, the old woodcarver, walked into the shop. Although his name was Geppetto, the neighborhood boys often called him Polenta because Geppetto's yellow wig reminded the boys of a kind of porridge made from cornmeal. It was a nickname that drove him wild. "Good

morning, Mister Cherry," Geppetto said. "Why are you sitting on the floor?"

"I am giving the ants a lesson about the alphabet," Mister Cherry said. "What can I do for you today?"

The carpenter got up off the floor as Geppetto explained his visit.

"I want to make a wooden puppet that will be able to dance and to do somersaults. I'm going to take it around the world so I can earn my living. How does that sound?" Geppetto asked.

"Good idea, Polenta," was the response. The voice didn't come from Mister Cherry, but Geppetto thought that it had. Geppetto was enraged that his good friend would call him by that awful nickname.

"Why have you insulted me?" asked Geppetto.

"It wasn't me," Mister Cherry cried.

"Yes, it was!" Geppetto said.

"No!" Mister Cherry said. Soon, the old friends were wrestling. When they were through, Geppetto had Mister Cherry's gray wig in his teeth, and Mister Cherry was wearing Geppetto's yellow wig.

Regaining their senses, they gave each other back their wigs. They made a promise not to ever have such a quarrel again.

"Now, Geppetto, what can I do for you?" Mister Cherry asked.

"I want a piece of wood to make my new puppet. Do you have one?" he asked.

At once, Mister Cherry went to get

the talking piece of wood that had startled him earlier. Just as Mister Cherry was about to hand the wood to Geppetto, it began to shake wildly in his hands. As it did, it struck poor Geppetto in the shins.

"Ouch! You clumsy ox, what did you do that for?" Geppetto asked.

"I didn't do anything. It was the wood," Mister Cherry said.

Geppetto and Mister Cherry went at it again. Each accused the other until they were wrestling on the floor of the wood-working shop again. After the battle, Mister Cherry had a few scratches on his nose and Geppetto had lost a few buttons from his sweater. They shook hands and again promised never to get into such an argument.

Geppetto got to his feet, picked up the piece of wood, and walked home.

CHAPTER 2

A Mind of Its Own

Geppetto's home was a small room with just a chair, a bed, and a broken-down table. There was a fireplace, but the fire in it wasn't real. It was a painting. There was a simmering saucepan that had a cloud of smoke coming from it. But that was a painting, too. Although Geppetto was poor, he made do with the little he had.

As soon as Geppetto was home, he took out his tools. First he named the future puppet "Pinocchio." Then he made the puppet's hair, forehead, and eyes. As soon as Geppetto finished the eyes,

they began to move and to look at him. Geppetto was astonished, but he kept working.

He shaped the nose, but when he was done it began to grow longer and longer. No matter what Geppetto did to shorten it, it continued to grow. When Geppetto shaped the puppet's mouth, it began to smile, then to laugh. Geppetto was annoyed. "What are you laughing at, you naughty puppet?" he asked. The puppet stopped laughing, but it stuck out its tongue. Geppetto pretended not to notice and kept working.

As soon as Geppetto finished the puppet's hands, his wig was suddenly pulled off of his head! "You should have respect for your father," Geppetto told the puppet.

Geppetto finished making Pinocchio by carving his legs and feet. As he did, he received a kick on the tip of his nose! "I deserve it!" Geppetto said

to himself. "I should have known this would happen."

In no time at all, Pinocchio started to walk all around the room. Before Geppetto could stop him, Pinocchio ran out the door, jumped into the street, and escaped.

"Stop him, stop him, stop him!" shouted Geppetto to the people in the street. But no one helped Geppetto. Everyone just stood still, watched and laughed. Only a policeman tried to help.

Pinocchio was about to run under the policeman's legs. But the policeman grabbed Pinocchio by his very long nose and handed him over to Geppetto.

Pinocchio knew Geppetto was going to punish him once he got home. So he threw himself on the ground in a tantrum. The crowd of people thought that Geppetto was a cruel man and made a fuss on Pinocchio's behalf. The policeman let Pinocchio go and took Geppetto off to jail.

"You wretched puppet," Geppetto grumbled. "To think of all the trouble I went through, to turn you into a nice puppet. I should have known this would happen."

CHAPTER 3
The Talking Cricket

While Geppetto was being taken off to prison, Pinocchio ran as fast as he could across the fields to get back home.

Once there, Pinocchio sat happily on the floor. All of a sudden, he heard a strange noise that made him sit up and look all around the room. "Who's that?" he asked, frightened.

"Cric, cric, cric, it's me," came the reply.

Pinocchio saw a big cricket crawling slowly up the wall. "Who are you?" he asked.

"I'm the Talking Cricket that's lived

in this room for more than one hundred years," the Cricket said.

"Well, please leave, this is my room now," Pinocchio said.

"I can't leave until I tell you something important, Pinocchio," the Cricket said.

"What can that be?" Pinocchio asked.

"Boys who turn against their parents and run away from home for no reason never come to any good. They will soon be sorry for their wild ways," the Cricket said.

"I don't believe that. I already decided to run away from here early tomorrow. If I stay, I know I'll have to go to school just like all the other boys. I don't want to learn. I just want to have fun," Pinocchio said to the Talking Cricket.

"You're a silly boy, Pinocchio. Don't you know that if you do that you'll grow up to be as dumb as a donkey?" the Cricket added.

"Oh, go away, Talking Cricket," Pinocchio said rudely.

"You should at least learn a trade so you can make a living," the Cricket advised.

But Pinocchio would have none of the Cricket's advice.

"The only trade for me is to eat, drink, sleep, and have fun all night and day," Pinocchio said.

"Poor, poor Pinocchio. I feel sorry for you," lamented the good-hearted Cricket. "You have a head made out of wood and don't know any better."

At the Talking Cricket's last remark, Pinocchio became very angry. He threw a hammer at him. The good-intentioned Cricket was suddenly done for.

CHAPTER 4
Pinocchio Burns His Feet

As nighttime approached, Pinocchio became hungry. He had to find something to eat. He ran to the fireplace to look into the saucepan, but he discovered that the fireplace was only a painting. Pinocchio ran around the room searching everywhere. He looked in all of the cabinets and drawers, but he could not find anything. Growing tired and weak, Pinocchio began to yawn again and again.

Pinocchio felt as if he would soon faint. He began to cry. "The Talking Cricket was right. I should never have turned against my father. If only my father were here now, I would not be so hungry. Hunger is an awful illness," he sobbed.

Then Pinocchio saw something in the dust heap. It was round and white. It was an egg.

"How shall I cook this egg?" he wondered. "An omelet would be tasty, or I could fry it, or boil it—whatever is the fastest," he decided.

But when Pinocchio broke the eggshell over the pan, a little chick popped out.

"Thank you so much, Pinocchio. You saved me the trouble of cracking the shell. Take care until we meet again," the little bird chirped as it flew out the window.

Pinocchio stood with his mouth open and his eyes staring, holding the bits of eggshell in his hands. "How

right the Talking Cricket was! If only I had not run away from home, and if only my dear father were here, I would not be all alone and so hungry."

Pinocchio decided to go out and to explore the neighborhood. He hoped to meet a kind person who would give him something to eat.

Pinocchio went outside into the stormy winter night. Thunder and lightning seemed to set the sky on fire.

Pinocchio was very afraid of thunder and lightning, but his hunger was stronger than his fear. He rushed toward town. He ran so fast that he was panting by the time he reached the small village.

Despairingly, Pinocchio pulled the bell rope of the first house he came to.

"Who is it?" a voice called from a small window above Pinocchio. "What do you want at this late hour?"

"Would you kindly give me a piece of bread, sir?" Pinocchio asked.

"I'll be back in a moment," the man said. He was certain that his caller was one of the troublesome boys who always rang the bell and then ran off. They always disturbed people in their homes. "Wait there," he said.

Pinocchio did as he was told. After a few minutes the window was opened again and the man said, "Stand under the window."

Then the man poured an entire bucket of water down on Pinocchio! The puppet was drenched.

Tired, hungry, and soaked, Pinocchio returned home, where he placed his feet on the coals to dry and warm them.

Pinocchio soon fell fast asleep. His wooden feet smoldered without his even knowing it. Pinocchio didn't awaken until daybreak, when someone knocked at the door.

"Who is it?" he asked, rubbing the sleep from his eyes.

"Your father, Geppetto!" was the response.

CHAPTER 5

A Spelling Book

"Open the door!" shouted Geppetto from the street.

"But Papa, I can't. My feet have been eaten!" Pinocchio cried as he stumbled to the floor.

"Who has eaten your feet?" Geppetto asked.

Pinocchio blamed the cat.

"Pinocchio, open the door at once," Geppetto shouted in frustration. He was sure this excuse was only another one of the puppet's tricks. Geppetto angrily climbed in through a window. When he saw his little puppet without feet, he was overcome with emotion.

"Pinocchio, how did you manage to burn your feet?" he asked.

"I don't know, Papa, it has been an awful night," Pinocchio said as he told Geppetto about the flying chick, the old man who threw water on him, and how he put his feet on the coals to dry. At the end of his sad tale, Pinocchio began to cry so loudly that he could be heard five miles away.

Geppetto saw that the puppet was dying of hunger. He took three pears from his pocket and gave them to Pinocchio. "Here, Pinocchio, these were for my breakfast, but you can have them. I hope they will make you feel better," Geppetto said.

"Please peel them for me," Pinocchio requested.

"Peel them?" Geppetto asked in disbelief. "I don't think you should be so picky when you're starving, Pinocchio," Geppetto suggested. "In this world, my boy, we should eat everything, for anything may happen to us."

"I'm sure you are right, Papa, but please peel them. I don't like the skin of the pear," Pinocchio said.

Geppetto picked up a knife and peeled the three pears, putting the skins on a corner of the table.

Pinocchio ate the first pear in two mouthfuls and was about to throw away the core. Geppetto stopped him and said, "Don't throw it away. You may want it later."

"I'm not going to eat the core!" the puppet shouted bitterly.

Geppetto only repeated what he had said earlier. "Who knows what life may bring, Pinocchio. Anything may happen to us in this world," he cautioned patiently. So the cores were placed on the corner of the table with the pear skins.

After devouring the three pears, Pinocchio was still hungry.

"I have nothing more to give you," Geppetto said.

"Nothing at all?" the puppet asked.

"Only the skins and the cores," Geppetto offered.

"Oh, well, I see that I must have patience," said Pinocchio. "If there is nothing else, I will eat them."

Pinocchio made faces as he chewed the skins and cores of the pears, but finally said, "Ah, now I feel better."

"You see," Geppetto said, "I was right. You shouldn't be too particular. Anything can happen to us in this world!"

Pinocchio wanted a new pair of feet. Geppetto, to punish him for being naughty, let him cry and moan for half the day.

"Why should I make new feet for you? You'll only run away from home again."

"I promise that I will go to school and I will study and do well," Pinocchio said.

"All boys, when they want something, say the same thing," Geppetto said.

"But I am not like other boys. I promise you, Papa, that I will learn a trade and that I will take care of you in your old age," Pinocchio said solemnly.

Geppetto tried to look stern. But his eyes were full of tears and his heart was full of sorrow at seeing his poor Pinocchio without feet. He picked up his tools and two small pieces of wood and started working.

"Close your eyes and go to sleep, Pinocchio," Geppetto said. Pinocchio shut his eyes and pretended to sleep while Geppetto glued his feet in place.

Then Pinocchio jumped down from the table and hugged Geppetto. Then he began to run all around the room.

"To reward you for what you have done for me," Pinocchio said, "I will go to school at once."

"Good boy," Geppetto said happily.

"But if I'm going to school, I'll need clothes," Pinocchio said.

Geppetto was poor and didn't have enough money to buy new clothes for Pinocchio. So he made Pinocchio a shirt of flowered paper and a pair of shoes from the bark of a tree. He also made a hat out of dough.

"I look like such a gentleman," Pinocchio said proudly, looking at his reflection in a basin of water.

"Yes, you do," answered Geppetto. "Keep in mind that it is not fine clothes that make a gentleman, but clean clothes."

"I forgot the most important thing of all," Pinocchio said.

"What is that?" Geppetto asked.

"I need a spelling book," the puppet said.

"But we don't have any money," Geppetto said.

Pinocchio became very sad.

"Don't worry, Pinocchio," Geppetto said. He put on his old coat and ran out the door.

Not long afterward, Geppetto returned holding a spelling book in his hand. The poor man was not wearing his coat, even though it was snowing outside.

"Papa, where is your coat?"

Pinocchio asked.

"I have sold it," Geppetto said.

"Why?" Pinocchio asked.

"Because it was too hot," Geppetto answered.

Pinocchio understood at once. Geppetto had sold his coat to get enough money to buy Pinocchio his spelling book. The puppet jumped up and hugged Geppetto.

CHAPTER 6
A Puppet Show

As soon as it stopped snowing, Pinocchio went to school. "I will learn to read, write, and count," Pinocchio said to himself. "Someday I will earn a lot of money and I'll buy a beautiful coat for my papa. It will be made of gold and silver and will have diamond buttons. My papa deserves it for buying me my spelling book."

While he was daydreaming, he thought he heard the sound of fifes and drums in the distance. "What can that music be?" Pinocchio wondered. "Too bad I have to go to school or I'd—"

Pinocchio had to make a decision.

Should he go to school or try to find out where the music was coming from?

"Today, I will go and hear the music and tomorrow I will go to school," he finally decided, running toward the sound of the fifes and drums.

"What is that building?" Pinocchio asked a little boy when he reached the town.

"Read the sign," the boy replied.

"I would read it if I could, but I don't know how to read yet," Pinocchio said.

"Okay, I will read it to you. It says, 'GREAT PUPPET THEATER,'" the boy said.

"Has the play started?" Pinocchio asked.

"It is just starting now," the boy told him.

"How much does it cost to go in?" Pinocchio asked.

"Two coins," the boy said.

Pinocchio was very curious to see the show. Without any shame, Pinocchio

asked the boy if he would lend him the money.

"I would lend the money to you happily, but it just so happens that today I cannot give it to you," the boy said.

"I will sell you my jacket," the puppet said.

"What would I do with a jacket made of flowered paper?" the boy asked the puppet.

"Will you buy my shoes or hat?" Pinocchio asked.

"There's a bargain! Shoes I could use to light a fire and a hat the mice would eat!" the boy teased.

Pinocchio was dismayed. "What will you give me for my spelling book?" he asked.

"I will buy the spelling book for two coins," a street vendor called out.

So Pinocchio sold the book right there and then. Imagine that at that very moment poor Geppetto was home trembling with cold in his shirtsleeves so that his ungrateful son could have a spelling book!

CHAPTER 7
The Puppet Theater

When Pinocchio entered the theater, the curtain was already up. Harlequin and Punchinello, two of the puppets, were quarreling, and the audience was laughing. Then Harlequin saw Pinocchio.

"Am I dreaming?" he asked. "Can it be Pinocchio?" (All puppets know one another, even if they have never met!)

"It is I," said Pinocchio.

"Pinocchio, it can't be," Rosa screamed, the lady puppet, looking out from behind the stage.

"It's Pinocchio!" all the puppets cried

at once.

Harlequin invited Pinocchio to come on stage and be welcomed by all the puppets. Pinocchio leaped from the back of the theater, climbing over the chairs and balancing on the head of the conductor, before he finally reached the stage. The hugging and cheers went on until the audience became impatient and began to shout, "We want the play!"

Instead, the puppets increased their noise and welcomed Pinocchio. They

raised him onto their shoulders and carried him in front of the footlights.

Just then, the manager, Fire-eater, came out wondering what all the fuss was about. He was very frightening. His beard was as black as ink, and so long that it reached from his chin to the ground. He even stepped on it as he walked! His mouth was huge, and his eyes glowed like burning flames. He carried a large whip that he cracked as he walked along.

When he appeared, silence suddenly fell over the theater. The puppets and the audience trembled.

"Why are you making trouble?" he Pinocchio asked in a terrible voice.

"It was not my fault, Your Honor," Pinocchio said.

"That's enough. I'll fix you later," the manager growled as he threatened Pinocchio.

As soon as the play had ended, Fire-eater went into a kitchen, where a lamb dinner was being prepared for

him. It turned on the spit in front of the fire, but the blaze wasn't big enough to cook the meat. He called Harlequin and Punchinello into the kitchen. "Bring me that puppet. He's made of wood dry enough to make a fine fire for cooking my dinner," he ordered.

Harlequin and Punchinello didn't want to put Pinocchio on the fire, but one look at their master's angry, fierce face and they obeyed.

When they returned with Pinocchio, he was screaming, "Papa, save me!"

When Fire-eater saw poor Pinocchio struggling and screaming, he began to feel sorry for him. He tried to hold out, but after a little while he sneezed. Whenever Fire-eater was overcome with emotion, he sneezed. It showed that he had a heart.

After he sneezed, however, he still pretended to be angry. "Stop crying. Your tears have given me a very funny feeling in my tummy. I feel such a pain that...that I...ah-ah-ah-choo!" he sneezed.

"Bless you," Pinocchio said.

"Thank you, little puppet. Where are your papa and mama?" he asked Pinocchio.

"I never knew my mama, but I miss my papa," Pinocchio said seriously.

"How sad your poor father would be if I had you thrown onto those burning coals. I feel for him . . . ah-choo, ah-choo, ah-choo," he sneezed again three times.

"Bless you," Pinocchio said again.

"Thank you. I deserve some pity, too, you know," Fire-eater said. "I have no wood to finish roasting my dinner. I'll burn one of the other puppets instead. Guards, guards, come here!"

Two wooden guards appeared. They were very tall and thin, wore hats, and held swords in their hands. "Take Harlequin, tie him up, and throw him on the fire. I want my dinner to be well roasted!" Fire-eater yelled.

Harlequin was so terrified that he fell on the ground.

"Have pity, Your Excellency!" Pinocchio pleaded.

Being called "Your Excellency" made Fire-eater very happy. He smiled and became kinder. "What do you want from me?" he asked Pinocchio.

"Spare poor Harlequin," begged Pinocchio.

"There is no mercy here. I must throw him on the fire. I want my lamb well roasted!" Fire-eater replied.

"In that case," Pinocchio cried, "throw me on the fire."

Pinocchio's heroic words made all of the puppets cry—even the guards.

Then Fire-eater sneezed four or five more times. He opened his arms and said to Pinocchio, "You are a good, brave boy! Come here and give me a kiss."

Pinocchio ran toward him at once

and climbed up Fire-eater's beard. When he reached the top, Pinocchio kissed him on the nose.

"Am I pardoned?" Harlequin asked shakily.

"Tonight I must eat my lamb half-cooked," said Fire-eater. "But next time, beware!"

All the puppets ran to the stage. They lit all the lamps and gave a full performance. At dawn, they were all still clapping and dancing.

CHAPTER 8

The Fox and the Cat

The next day, Fire-eater gave Pinocchio five gold coins to give to Geppetto. Pinocchio thanked Fire-eater a thousand times and left to return home.

On the way he met a lame Fox and a blind Cat.

"Hello, Pinocchio," the Fox said.

"How do you know my name?" Pinocchio asked.

"I know your father," the Fox replied.

"When did you see him?" Pinocchio asked.

"I saw him yesterday. He was in his shirtsleeves shivering," the Fox replied.

"Poor Papa," sighed Pinocchio. "But he won't be cold much longer because I am rich now."

The Fox and the Cat began to laugh—until Pinocchio showed them the gold coins.

The Fox stretched out the paw that was supposed to be lame, and the Cat opened both of her eyes, then shut them again so quickly that Pinocchio didn't see it.

"What are you going to do with all

that money?" the Fox asked.

"First, I am going to buy a new coat for my papa. Then I'll buy a new spelling book for me," Pinocchio told them.

"For you?" the Fox asked.

"For you?" the Cat repeated.

"Yes, I really want to go to school and to learn," the puppet said.

"But studying has made me lame," the Fox said.

"And studying has made me blind," the Cat said.

"Don't listen to the advice of bad companions, Pinocchio," said a blackbird sitting on a branch.

But the Cat jumped onto the poor bird and ate him in one bite to teach the bird a lesson about minding his own business.

"Pinocchio, would you like to double your money?" the Fox asked.

"How?" Pinocchio asked.

"Instead of going home, come with us to Fools Town," the Fox said.

"No, I can't," Pinocchio said. "I must return to my papa."

"Think about it, Pinocchio. You're giving up a fortune," the Fox said.

"Yes, a fortune, "the Cat said.

"How is that possible?" Pinocchio asked.

"There is a special field in Fools Town

that everyone calls the Field of Riches. First, you dig a small hole and put a coin into it. You cover the hole with some dirt. Then you water it and go away. When you return, you find a fortune," the Fox explained.

Pinocchio was giddy at the thought. "As soon as I have a fortune," Pinocchio said, "I will give you some money as a present."

"A present for us!" the Fox said as if he were offended. "What are you dreaming of? We would never take your money!"

"What are you dreaming of?" the Cat asked again, shaking her head.

Then and there Pinocchio forgot all about his resolution to be good and to go to school. How good these two are, he thought. Pinocchio decided to go with the Fox and Cat to Fools Town.

CHAPTER 9

The Inn of
the Red Starfish

"Let's stop here for a little while," the Fox said when they reached the Inn of the Red Starfish.

The Fox, the Cat, and Pinocchio entered the inn and sat down at a table, even though they weren't hungry.

The Cat, who had an upset stomach, could only eat thirty-five fish with tomato sauce and four portions of tripe with Parmesan cheese. After complaining that the tripe was not well seasoned, she asked for more butter and cheese!

The Fox, who was on a strict diet, had to be satisfied with sweet-and-sour duck and side dishes of chicken and rabbit. After eating the duck, the Fox asked for a special dish of pheasants, frogs, lizards, and other delicacies. After that, he could not touch anything else!

Of the three, Pinocchio ate the least. He asked for nuts and bread and left everything on his plate. The poor boy was thinking only of the Field of Riches.

After they finished their meal, the Fox asked the host of the inn for two

rooms, one for Pinocchio and one for himself and the Cat.

Pinocchio had just gone to bed and started dreaming of making a fortune when he heard a loud knocking at his door. The innkeeper had come to tell him that it was midnight.

"Are my friends ready to go?" the puppet asked.

"Ready! They left two hours ago," the innkeeper said. "They will wait for you at the Field of Riches at daybreak."

Pinocchio gave the innkeeper a gold coin for his and his friends' supper. Then he left the inn.

The countryside was very dark. As Pinocchio walked along, he saw a little insect shining on the trunk of a tree. "Who are you?" Pinocchio asked.

"I am the ghost of the Talking Cricket," the insect answered.

"What do you want?" Pinocchio asked.

"I want to give you advice, Pinocchio. Take the four gold coins you still have left and bring them to your poor father. He is so sad that you have never returned to him," the ghost said.

"My papa will be a rich man tomorrow," Pinocchio told the ghost of the Cricket.

"My boy, don't trust those who promise to make you rich in a day. Listen to me and go back home," the ghost of the Cricket warned.

"Nonsense," the puppet said. "I will go to the Field of Riches."

"Remember, boys who are determined to have their own way and only want to please themselves are sorry for it sooner or later," the ghost of the Cricket said.

"You always have the same old worries! Good night, ghost of the Cricket," Pinocchio said.

"Good night, Pinocchio," the ghost of the Cricket said. "May you be safe from all danger and assassins."

As soon as the ghost of the Cricket said those words, he vanished into the dark night.

"Really!" Pinocchio said to himself as he continued walking. "We poor boys—everyone wants to tell us what to do. These stories of assassins were invented by papas just to frighten boys who want to go out at night!"

CHAPTER 10

Pinocchio Meets Assassins

Suddenly Pinocchio heard a rustle of leaves behind him. He turned to look and saw, in the gloomy darkness, two evil-looking figures completely covered in black sacks. They were running after him on tiptoe.

"Oh, no! Here they really are!" Pinocchio said to himself. Not knowing where to hide his gold coins, he put them into his mouth just under his tongue.

Pinocchio tried to escape, but he had not gone a step when he was grabbed by the arm and heard two terrible voices saying to him, "Your money or your life!"

Pinocchio could not answer, so he gestured with his head and hands as if to say, "I don't have any money."

"Give us the money or you're done for," the taller robber said.

"Done for," the smaller one repeated.

"And after we're done with you, we'll get your father, too," the taller thief said.

"Your father, too," the smaller one repeated.

"No, not my poor papa!" cried Pinocchio. As he cried out, the gold coins clinked in his mouth.

"Ah! You rascal, you've hidden your money under your tongue. Spit it out at once!" the thief demanded.

Pinocchio wouldn't do it.

Then the shorter assassin tried to pry Pinocchio's lips open. But Pinocchio, who was quick, bit off the assassin's hand and spat it out. To his surprise, Pinocchio saw that he spat out a cat's paw!

Once he was free, Pinocchio ran as fast as he could. The assassins ran after him. The one who had lost a paw ran on only three legs!

After running a few miles, Pinocchio was exhausted. He climbed a very high pine tree and sat on the topmost branch. The assassins tried to climb up after him but couldn't, so they collected dry wood and piled it under the pine and set it on fire. Pinocchio jumped from the top of the tree and started to run across the fields again. The two assassins followed.

At daybreak, the assassins were still

chasing Pinocchio when he reached a ditch full of dirty water. Pinocchio jumped across it to the other side. The assassins also jumped but they fell into the middle of the ditch.

To Pinnochio's surprise, they were still running after him even though they were dripping with dirty water.

After seeing the thieves chasing him again, Pinocchio was almost at the point of giving up. He looked in every direction and saw a small white house hidden in the woods.

He arrived out of breath at the door of the house and knocked. No one answered. He knocked again harder because he heard the assassins approaching. There was still no answer!

In desperation, Pinocchio began to kick the door. At that, a lovely little girl came to the window. She had blue hair and a face as white as wax. Her hands were crossed on her chest. Without moving her lips at all, she said in a soft little voice, "There is no one here. They are all dead."

"Open the door yourself, then," the puppet cried.

"I am dead, too," the little girl said.

"Then what are you doing talking to me at the window?" Pinocchio asked.

"I am waiting for the hearse to take me away," was the reply. Having said this, the girl disappeared, and silently the window closed.

"Oh, beautiful little girl with blue hair," Pinocchio cried, "pity me and open the door. I am being chased by—"

But Pinocchio couldn't finish his words. Someone suddenly grabbed him by the collar. The same two horrible voices from before said, "You won't escape from us again!"

The puppet, seeing no way to escape, was trembling so much that his wooden joints creaked and the gold coins clinked under his tongue.

"Now then," the assassins demanded,

"will you open your mouth? If not we'll just force you to open it."

Luckily for Pinocchio, since he was made of very hard wood, nothing they tried worked.

"I know what we must do," one voice said. "We must tie him to that tree!"

"To that tree," the other repeated.

Without losing any time, they tied Pinocchio's arms behind him, put a rope around him, and tied him to an oak tree.

"We'll come back tomorrow," they said

as they walked off.

Pinocchio never gave up hope that some passerby would help him. But no one came, and Pinocchio began to think of his poor father. "Oh, Papa, if only you were here," he said, sighing.

The lovely little girl with blue hair—who was really a Fairy—came back to the window and in a distance saw Pinocchio tied to the tree. She felt compassion for him and sent a large Falcon to the tree to untie Pinocchio.

Then the Fairy clapped twice, and a magnificent Poodle, walking upright like a man, appeared in her room.

The Poodle was dressed as a coachman. "Be quick, Medoro, like a good dog!" the Fairy said to the Poodle. "Bring out the most beautiful carriage in my coach house and take the road to the woods. When you come to the oak tree you'll find a poor puppet lying in the grass. Bring him here to me."

Not fifteen minutes had passed when

the carriage returned. The Fairy took the poor puppet in her arms and carried him into a little room. Then the Fairy called three doctors. They were a Crow, an Owl, and a Cricket.

"Gentlemen," the Fairy said, "I want to know if this puppet is alive or dead."

"I have seen this puppet before," the Cricket said. "He is a scoundrel!"

Pinocchio opened his eyes, then shut them immediately again, squirming around under the covers.

"That puppet is a disobedient boy,

a bad son who broke his poor father's heart!" the Cricket continued.

Pinocchio began to cry.

"When a dead person cries, it is a sign that he is going to recover," the Crow announced to the others.

"No," the Owl said, "when a dead person cries, it's a sign that he is sorry to die."

CHAPTER 11
Pinocchio's Nose Grows

As soon as the three doctors left, the Fairy gave Pinocchio a glass of water with medicine in it.

"Is it sweet or bitter?" Pinocchio asked.

"It is bitter, but it will make you feel better. Drink it and then I'll give you a lump of sugar to take the bitter taste away," the Fairy said.

"First give me the lump of sugar," Pinocchio said.

"Do you promise you'll take your medicine, Pinocchio?" the Fairy asked.

"Yes," the puppet said.

The Fairy gave Pinocchio the sugar and he quickly chewed and swallowed it.

"Now, Pinocchio, keep your promise," the Fairy said.

Pinocchio took the glass unhappily and put it up to his nose, then to his lips, then to his nose again.

Suddenly Pinocchio burst out, "I will not drink that bitter water. I just won't!"

"You will be sorry," the Fairy said. "In a few hours your fever will be very high."

"I don't care," he insisted. "I'd rather die than drink that bitter water."

"You will surely die if you don't take the medicine," the Fairy said.

Pinocchio did not want to die. He was so scared that he gulped down the entire glass of medicine water in no time! A few minute later, Pinocchio jumped down from the bed feeling quite well.

"My medicine has really helped you, Pinocchio," the Fairy said. "Why didn't you want to take it?"

"Taking medicine is worse than being sick," Pinocchio replied. "All boys know that!"

"Pinocchio, how did you meet those

assassins?" the Fairy asked.

Pinocchio told the Fairy about selling the spelling book to see the puppet show and how he met Fire-eater and the Fox and the Cat, and about the gold coins and the Field of Riches.

"Where are the gold coins now?" the Fairy asked.

"I lost them in the woods," he lied. Suddenly, his nose grew a few inches.

"If you lost the coins in the woods," the Fairy said, "we will find them."

"Oh, I remember, now," Pinocchio said. "I didn't lose them, I swallowed them

84

when I was drinking your medicine."

At this lie, Pinocchio's nose grew so long that he could not move in any direction. The Fairy looked at Pinocchio and laughed.

"Why are you laughing at me?" he asked, confused and unhappy to find his nose growing.

"I am laughing at the lies you have told, Pinocchio," she said.

"How do you know that I have lied?" he asked.

"Lies are found out immediately," the Fairy said. "Some lies have short legs, and some lies have long noses. Your lie is one that has a long nose."

Ashamed, Pinocchio tried to run out of the room. But he couldn't because his nose was too long to pass through the doorway!

CHAPTER 12
The Field of Riches

To teach Pinocchio a lesson, the Fairy let him cry for half the day before she summoned woodpeckers to fix his nose.

"What a good Fairy you are," Pinocchio said, drying his eyes. "I love you so much!"

"I love you, too," answered the Fairy. "If you will stay with me and be my good little brother, I'll be your sister."

"I will, but what about my poor papa?" Pinocchio asked.

"I have already let your father know, and he will be here tonight," the

Fairy replied.

"Really?" Pinocchio shouted. "I would like to go and meet him."

"Go ahead, but be careful not to get lost," the Fairy said.

Not far from the house, Pinocchio ran into the Fox and the Cat. "Well, well, here is our dear Pinocchio!" the Fox cried, kissing and hugging the puppet. "How is it that you are here, Pinocchio?"

"How is it that you are here?" the Cat mimicked.

While Pinocchio told them of the awful assassins and of being tied to a tree, he noticed that the Cat was lame and that she had lost her right front paw—claws and all.

The clever Fox, seeing this, abruptly said, "And what are you doing here now, Pinocchio?"

"I am waiting for my papa," the puppet answered.

"Where are your gold coins?" the Fox asked.

"I have them in my pocket. All but the one I spent at the Inn of the Red Starfish," Pinocchio said.

"Ah, to think that tomorrow, instead of four gold pieces, they could become two thousand!" the Fox said. "Why don't you listen to my advice and go and bury them in the Field of Riches?"

"Not today," Pinocchio said. "I will go another day."

"Another day will be too late!" the Fox exclaimed.

"Too late," the Cat repeated.

"Why?" Pinocchio asked.

"Because the field has been bought by a nobleman and after tomorrow no one will be allowed to bury money there," the Fox said.

"How far away is the Field of Riches?" the puppet asked.

"Less than two miles—will you come with us?" the Fox asked.

Pinocchio thought of the good Fairy and of old Geppetto and of the warnings of the Talking Cricket. He hesitated for a few moments. In the end, since he had no common sense at all, he shouted, "I will go!"

After walking half the day, they reached Fools Town. The streets were crowded with hungry animals. Pinocchio saw sheep shorn and shivering from cold, roosters without combs or head crests, and disheveled dogs all begging for food.

"We are here," the Fox said when they

arrived at an ordinary field. "Now bend down and dig a hole with your hands to put your gold coins in. Then cover it up with dirt."

Pinocchio did as the Fox said.

"Now, go to that stream and get some

water. Then water the ground where you have buried the gold coins," the Fox directed.

Pinocchio did so and asked, "What else do I have to do?"

"Nothing else," the Fox answered.

"Now we can go away. You can return in about twenty minutes and you'll find a plant with its branches filled with money."

Pinocchio was overjoyed. He thanked the Fox and the Cat and promised them a beautiful present.

"We don't want any presents," the devious Fox said. "Teaching you how to become rich without working for it is enough for us."

Then they all went their separate ways.

CHAPTER 13

Robbed and Sent to Prison

Pinocchio was dreaming of all the things he'd spend his money on as he walked back to the field later that day. "I'll have a palace, wooden horses, stables full of candies, cakes and lots more!" he said to himself.

When he reached the field, he went right up to the tiny hole where he had buried his gold coins. Nothing had grown there.

At that moment, he heard loud laughing close by. Looking up, he saw a large Parrot perched on a tree.

"Why are you laughing?" Pinocchio

angrily asked.

"I am laughing at the fools who believe in all the silly things that are told to them," the Parrot answered.

"Are you talking about me?" asked Pinocchio.

"Yes, I am, poor Pinocchio," the Parrot said. "Do you really believe that money can be grown with dirt and water? I believed it once, and today, I am suffering for it."

"I don't understand you," Pinocchio said, trembling with fear.

"While you were in town, the Fox and the Cat came back to the field. They took the money you buried, and left," the Parrot told him.

Pinocchio stood with his mouth open, not wanting to believe the Parrot's words. He began digging again. The hole was deep, but the money was no longer there.

Pinocchio ran back to town and went to the courts to file a complaint against

the Fox and the Cat. The judge was an old gorilla with a white beard. He was very respectable and wore gold-rimmed spectacles without glass in them. Pinocchio told his story and demanded justice.

The judge listened patiently. When Pinocchio had nothing further to say, the judge rang a bell. Two dogs, dressed as policemen, appeared.

"That poor puppet has been robbed. Take him to prison," ordered the judge. Pinocchio was shocked as he was dragged off to jail.

Pinocchio remained in prison for four months. Finally, the young Emperor who reigned over Fools Town won a victory against his enemies. He was so happy that he ordered all prisoners be set free.

CHAPTER 14

A Farmer's Watchdog

Without delay, Pinocchio left the prison and took the road that led to the Fairy's house. Because of the rainy weather, the road had become muddy and Pinocchio sank into the mud. But he wouldn't give up his effort to see the Fairy again.

"So many misfortunes have happened to me," he said to himself as he went along. "I deserved them. Will the Fairy forgive me for my bad behavior? She was so kind and loving. I owe her my life! Could there ever be a more ungrateful boy than me?"

Soon Pinocchio began to get very hungry. So he jumped into a field on the side of the road to pick some grapes.

He had hardly reached the vines when his leg was caught in a trap set to capture the polecats—small animals that liked to eat eggs and chickens.

By nighttime, Pinocchio began to cry both from the pain of the trap cutting his legs and from fear at being alone in the dark in the middle of the fields.

Just at that moment, a Firefly flew over his head. He called to it for help.

"Poor puppet!" the Firefly said, as he stopped near Pinocchio. "How did your legs get caught in the trap?"

"I went into the field to pick some grapes, and—" Pinocchio began.

"But were the grapes yours to pick?" the Firefly asked.

"No," Pinocchio answered.

"Who taught you to take things from people?" the Firefly asked.

"I was hungry," Pinocchio said.

"Hunger isn't a reason to take what isn't yours," the Firefly said.

"I will never do it again," Pinocchio said, crying.

Their conversation was interrupted by the sound of approaching footsteps. It was the owner of the field coming on tiptoe to see if he had caught any polecats in his trap.

"Ah, a thief!" the angry farmer said. "So you're the one who takes my chickens!"

"No!" Pinocchio cried. "I only came into the field to take some grapes!"

"A grape thief can also be a chicken thief," the farmer said.

The farmer opened the trap and grabbed Pinocchio by his collar. When he reached the yard in front of the house, he threw Pinocchio on the ground.

"We'll sort this out tomorrow," the farmer said. "In the meantime, you'll be my watchdog tonight." He strapped a huge dog collar around Pinocchio's neck. It was attached to the wall with a chain. He ordered Pinocchio to bark if he saw robbers. Then he left.

Pinocchio cried, "It serves me right! If only I could start over again. But it

is too late."

After his outburst, Pinocchio felt better and went into the kennel and fell asleep.

Pinocchio was sleeping for two hours when he heard voices in the yard. Peering from the kennel, he saw four animals with dark fur. They were polecats!

"Who are you?" one of the polecats asked.

"I'm Pinocchio," the puppet said.

"You're a puppet acting as a watchdog?" the polecat asked.

"Yes—as a punishment," Pinocchio said.

"I will offer you a deal," the polecat said. "You let us into this yard one night a week to take eight chickens. We'll keep seven and give you one for not alerting the farmer."

"It's a deal!" Pinocchio said.

Certain that they were safe, the four polecats entered the yard. No soon-

er were they inside than they heard the gate close. Pinocchio had trapped them. Then Pinocchio began to bark just like a watchdog!

The farmer came to the window. "What is the matter?" he asked.

"There are robbers in the poultry yard," Pinocchio said.

The farmer rushed into the yard. He caught the polecats and put them into a sack. "How did you discover these thieves?" the farmer asked.

Pinocchio told him the whole story. "I may be a puppet with many faults, but I will not make a deal with dishonest thieves!" Pinocchio proclaimed.

"Well done, my boy! As your reward, I'll set you free," the farmer said. He removed the collar from the puppet's neck.

CHAPTER 15

In Search of Geppetto

Pinocchio never stopped walking until he reached the road that led to the Fairy's house. Although he looked in every direction, the house that belonged to the little girl wasn't there.

Instead there was a marble stone that read:

"Here Lies the Little Girl with the Blue Hair Who Died from Sorrow Because She Was Abandoned by Pinocchio"

Pinocchio fell to the ground, crying in agony. "Oh, little Fairy, if you really love your little brother, come back to

"Here Lies the
Little Girl
with the Blue Hair
Who Died from
Sorrow Because
She Was
Abandoned
by Pinocchio"

life again," he cried.

Then a Pigeon flew over Pinocchio's head and asked, "Do you happen to know a puppet named Pinocchio?"

"I am Pinocchio," he said, jumping quickly to his feet.

"Do you also know Geppetto?" the Pigeon asked as he landed on the ground.

"He is my papa! Where is he? Is he still alive? Please answer me," Pinocchio begged.

"I left him three days ago. He was building a boat to cross the ocean to search for you," the Pigeon said. "If you wish to go, I'll carry you there."

Without waiting a moment, Pinocchio jumped onto the Pigeon's back. The pigeon took off, and they soared up to the clouds. Pinocchio was afraid of falling off.

After flying all day, they stopped for a rest and something to eat. They went into a deserted nest. All they found was a basin full of water and cabbage.

Pinocchio hated cabbage and refused to eat it. But, by nighttime, he was so hungry that he ate it all!

The following morning they reached the seashore. The Pigeon dropped off Pinocchio quickly and flew away.

The shore was crowded with many people looking toward the sea. "What has happened?" Pinocchio asked a woman.

"A man has gone to sea in search of his son," she said, pointing to a little

boat that was very far away.

"It's my papa!" Pinocchio screamed.

One moment the boat could be seen on the surface of a wave, the next it was out of sight. Pinocchio tried to get Geppetto's attention by waving his hat and making every kind of signal he could.

Geppetto seemed to recognize Pinocchio and began to row back to shore. Just then a tremendous wave rose, and the boat disappeared for good into the choppy water.

"Poor man," a fishermen sighed,

shaking his head.

"I'll save my papa!" Pinocchio shouted as he jumped from a rock into the swirling sea. Since he was made of wood and able to float, Pinocchio could swim, and he swam like a fish.

CHAPTER 16

Pinocchio Makes
a Promise

Pinocchio swam the whole night. It rained and hailed. The thunder and lightning were frightening.

At dawn, Pinocchio saw a long strip of land not far off from where he was swimming. It was an island in the middle of the sea. A big wave rose up with such force that it lifted him and threw him onto the sandy shore.

Little by little, the sky cleared and the sun began to shine. The sea became quiet again.

Pinocchio put his clothes in the sun to dry. He began to look all around in hopes of seeing the little boat with

Geppetto in it. He couldn't see anything except the sky and the ocean.

At that moment, a Dolphin swam by.

"Hello, Mister Fish," Pinocchio called. "Are there any villages on this island?"

"Yes, take the path to the left and follow your nose. You can't miss it," the nice Dolphin said.

"Tell me something else, please," Pinocchio continued. "Have you seen a little boat with my papa in it?"

"Who is your papa?" the dolphin asked.

"He is the best papa in the entire world, although I am the worst son," Pinocchio said sadly.

"The little boat must have gone to the bottom of the sea during the awful storm last night," the Dolphin said.

"What about my papa?" Pinocchio asked.

"He must have been swallowed up by the shark that has been swimming in these waters," the Dolphin said.

"Is the shark very big?" Pinocchio asked.

"Bigger than a five-story building," the Dolphin said.

Pinocchio was terrified. He quickly dressed and said good-bye to the kind dolphin. Then he rushed down the path.

Pinocchio soon reached a little village where all the people were hard at work. No one was lazy or idle.

"Ah," Pinocchio said, "this village

isn't for me. I wasn't born to work."

Pinocchio was starving, but he was ashamed to beg. At that moment a man, pulling two carts of coal, came down the road.

"Would you be kind enough to give me a coin so I can buy some food, sir?" Pinocchio asked.

"I'll give you two coins," the man said, "if you help me drag these two carts home."

"What? I am not used to working like a mule," Pinocchio said.

"Well, I hope your pride feeds your hunger," the man said. Then he walked

away.

A few minutes later a mason passed. He was carrying a basket of stones.

"Good man, would you give a coin to a poor boy who is hungry?" Pinocchio asked.

"Yes," answered the man. "Carry this basket for me and I'll give you five coins."

"But the basket is too heavy," Pinocchio grumbled.

"Well then, you'll have to remain hungry," the man said.

Finally a nice woman carrying two cans of water came by.

"May I have a drink of water from one of your cans?" Pinocchio asked, who was now very thirsty.

"Drink, my boy," the woman said.

Pinocchio drank. Then he said, "If only I could find something to eat."

With compassion, the woman said, "Help me carry these cans of water and I will give you a piece of bread."

Pinocchio looked at the cans and

didn't answer.

"I'll also give you a plate of vegetables," she said.

Pinocchio still didn't answer.

"Then I'll give you a nice dessert," the woman added.

Pinocchio couldn't resist. "I must have patience!" he said at last. "I will carry one of the cans to your house."

When they reached the house, Pinocchio sat at a small table that was already set. The woman gave him the bread, vegetables, and dessert.

Pinocchio devoured his meal. When he was finished eating, he raised his head to thank the woman. He looked at her with his eyes open wide and said, "Oh-h-h!"

"What is the matter?" the woman asked.

"You remind me of...! Oh, Fairy, is it really you?" Pinocchio cried. He hugged the little woman and began to cry.

Finally the little woman admitted she was the Fairy. "I was a child when you left me. Now I am almost old enough to be your mama," she said.

"How did you grow so fast?" Pinocchio asked.

"That's a secret," the Fairy said.

"Teach me to grow," he said.

"You can't grow because you are a puppet," the Fairy said.

"I am tired of being a puppet," Pinocchio cried. "I want to become a

man."

"You will, once you learn to be a good boy," the Fairy said.

"Am I not a good boy?" Pinocchio asked.

"Good boys are obedient, and you—" the Fairy said.

"I never obey," the puppet said.

"Good boys like to learn and to work, and you—" the Fairy said.

"I am lazy," the puppet said.

"Good boys always tell the truth, and you—" the Fairy said.

"I always tell lies," the puppet said.

"Good boys go to school, and you —" the Fairy said.

"I hate school," the puppet said. "But from today on, I'll go to school and work hard."

"Do you promise?" the Fairy asked.

"I promise. I will become a good little boy and I will help my papa," Pinocchio said. "Will I ever see him again?"

"I am very sure that you will see him again," the Fairy replied.

Pinocchio was so happy that he kissed the Fairy's hands. "Were you really dead?"

"It seems that I was not," the Fairy said, smiling.

"If only you knew the sorrow I felt and how it broke my heart," Pinocchio said, sighing.

"That is why I have forgiven you. I saw from your grief that you had a good heart. There is always hope that bad boys will change their ways to good.

That is why I came to look for you here. I would like nothing more than to be your mama," the Fairy said.

"That would be wonderful!" Pinocchio exclaimed.

"But you must be good and do everything that I tell you to do, Pinocchio," the Fairy instructed.

"I will," Pinocchio said.

"Tomorrow you will go to school with the other boys to learn a trade or craft," the Fairy said.

"But I don't want to learn a trade or craft," Pinocchio muttered.

"Why?" the Fairy asked.

"Because work makes me tired," Pinocchio said.

"Pinocchio," the Fairy said, "every man, whether he is born rich or poor, has to do something in this world. Laziness is a very bad habit that must be changed quickly before it is too late."

"I will do everything that you tell me to do, because I wish to become a boy,"

Pinocchio said. "You promised that I would become one, didn't you?"

"I did promise you that, Pinocchio. But it is all up to you now," the Fairy said.

CHAPTER 17

Pinocchio Skips School

The next day, Pinocchio went to school.

Imagine how happy all the little children were when they saw a puppet walk into the school! They laughed and played all kinds of tricks on him.

At first Pinocchio pretended not to care about their teasing. But he finally lost all of his patience and had a fight with some of the boys.

"I respect you, and you should respect me," Pinocchio said.

After this, Pinocchio and the children became friends.

The teacher liked Pinocchio because he was attentive and smart. Pinocchio was always the first at school in the morning and the last to leave in the afternoon.

But Pinocchio made many friends, and some of them were known for causing trouble. Every day the Fairy warned Pinocchio not to let the bad boys influence him in bad ways.

One day when Pinocchio was on his way to school, he met a few of his friends. "Have you heard the great news?" they asked him.

"No," Pinocchio answered.

"There's a shark as big as a mountain in the sea near here," they said.

Pinocchio wondered if it could be the same shark that was nearby when his poor papa drowned.

"We are going to see him. Do you want to come with us?" they asked.

"No, I'm going to school," Pinocchio answered.

"Why bother? We can go to school tomorrow," one of the boys said.

"But what will our teacher say?" Pinocchio asked.

"Who cares?" the boys asked.

"I will go see the shark when school is over," Pinocchio said.

"Do you think that the shark will wait for you?" one of the boys asked.

"Okay, then, let's go!" Pinocchio shouted. "Whoever gets there first is the best!"

They all rushed off across the fields with their books under their arms. Pinocchio was in the lead. Little did he know the trouble that awaited him.

"Where is the shark?" Pinocchio asked when they arrived at the shore.

"He must be having his breakfast," one of the boys teased.

From their laughter and jokes, Pinocchio knew that his school friends had made a fool of him. There was no shark. "Why do you think tricking me is so funny?" he asked.

"It's funny that you missed school," the boys said. "You make us look bad to the teacher because you are so good in school."

"What do you want me to do?" Pinocchio asked.

"Do the same things we do. Hate school, lessons, and the teacher—our three greatest enemies!" they shouted.

"But what if I want to learn?" Pinocchio asked.

"We'll have nothing more to do with you," one of them threatened.

"Is that so?" the puppet asked.

"We're not afraid of you," the biggest of the boys shouted. "There are seven of us against one of you."

They started fighting. Although Pinocchio was only one against seven, he defended himself like a hero.

The boys were furious that they could not beat Pinocchio. So they took out their school books and began throwing them at him. Pinocchio was able to duck

and always managed to avoid getting hit.

Having no more books of their own, the boys took a big book out of Pinocchio's backpack. One of them threw it at Pinocchio's head, but missed. The book hit one of the other boys. The boy turned white as a sheet and fell to the sand. The terrified boys ran away.

Even though he was frightened, Pinocchio stayed to help his school friend. "Eugene, open your eyes," Pinocchio cried. "What will I do? Oh, I should have gone to

school! Why did I listen to my friends? I am a stubborn fool. Now I have to suffer for it. What is to become of me?"

Pinocchio began to cry. Then he heard footsteps approaching. He turned and saw two policemen. They asked Pinocchio what happened. Although he said he did not hurt Eugene, when the policemen learned it was Pinocchio's book that struck the boy, they arrested him.

"But I'm innocent," Pinocchio said.

"Come with us," they demanded.

The policemen told some fishermen to take care of Eugene until they returned. Then they turned to Pinocchio, placed him between them, and said, "Walk quickly or you'll be sorry!"

Just as they reached the village, a great gust of wind blew Pinocchio's hat off his head. "May I go get my hat?" he asked.

"Go ahead, but hurry," they answered.

Pinocchio went to get his hat. Instead of getting it, he began to run as fast as he could back toward the seashore.

Thinking it would be hard to overtake Pinocchio, the policemen sent a huge dog after him. Pinocchio ran, but the dog, whose name was Alidoro, ran faster. Clouds of dust rose behind Pinocchio and the dog so that neither of them could be seen.

CHAPTER 18
The Green Fisherman

Alidoro had almost caught up with Pinocchio when the puppet reached the beach and jumped into the water. Alidoro couldn't stop in time and fell into the ocean. The poor dog couldn't swim, so he tried to keep himself afloat with his paws. The more he struggled, the farther he sank.

"Help me! Save me!" Alidoro begged.

Pinocchio, who really did have a very wonderful heart, felt compassion. He said, "I will save you if you promise not to chase me."

"I promise!" Alidoro said. "But hurry,

please!"

Pinocchio remembered that his father taught him that a good deed is always rewarded. So, he swam to Alidoro and brought him safely back to the beach.

Pinocchio didn't really trust the dog. So he jumped back into the water and swam away. "Good-bye, Alidoro. Good luck to you," he called from a safe distance.

"Good-bye, Pinocchio," the dog answered. "Thanks for saving my life."

Pinocchio kept swimming. Along the shore he saw a cave with a cloud of smoke rising from it. As he climbed the rocks, he felt something under the water rising higher and higher and carrying him into the air. He tried to escape, but it was too late. He was trapped with a swarm of fish of every size and shape in a big net. The fish were flapping and struggling to be set free.

Then, a fisherman came out of the cave. He looked like a sea monster with thick green grass on his head instead of hair. His skin was green, his eyes were green, and his long beard, which reached down to the ground, was also green.

The fisherman drew his net out of the water. "I'll have a feast of fish today!" he exclaimed.

"How lucky I am not a fish!" Pinocchio said to himself.

The fisherman carried the net full of fish into the cave.

"Now let's see what kind of fish these are!" the green fisherman said. He put his enormous hand into the net. He pulled out a handful of fish. Then he threw them into a pan without water.

The last fish in the net was Pinocchio!

The fisherman took Pinocchio out of the net. He looked at him and said, "This must be a crab."

"I am not a crab! I am a puppet!" Pinocchio exclaimed.

"A puppet?" the fisherman asked. "That's a new fish for me. I'll eat you with the greatest pleasure."

"Eat me? But I am not a fish. Don't you hear me talking just like you do?" Pinocchio asked.

"You are a fish that can talk and reason like me," the fisherman said. "You can decide how you would like to be cooked!"

Pinocchio began to cry and scream, begging the fisherman for mercy. "If only I had gone to school," he moaned.

Pinocchio tried to slip out of the green fisherman's hands. But it was useless. He threw Pinocchio in with the other fish. Then the fisherman took a wooden bowl full of flour and started to

139

flour each of the fish. As soon as they were ready, he threw them into the frying pan.

At last it was Pinocchio's turn. Pinocchio was so frightened, he couldn't move or speak. He was only able to beg for mercy with his scared little eyes! The green fisherman didn't care at all. He plunged him into the flour five times.

The fisherman was just about ready to throw Pinocchio into the frying pan when Alidoro entered the cave. The dog was drawn to the cave by the smell of the frying fish.

"Get out!" the fisherman shouted. But the dog was so hungry that he would not back down. Instead, he bared his fangs and growled.

"Save me, Alidoro!" Pinocchio cried.

Alidoro grabbed Pinocchio gently between his teeth and ran out of the cave. The furious fisherman couldn't catch the quick dog. Alidoro stopped running when he reached the path that led to the village.

"I have so much to thank you for," Pinocchio said.

"You saved me once, and one good turn deserves another," Alidoro replied.

Alidoro then took the road home. Pinocchio went to a nearby cottage, where he found out that his friend

Eugene had recovered from his injuries.

Then Pinocchio headed for the Fairy's house. "How can I ever show myself to her again?" he wondered. When he reached the Fairy's house his courage failed him at first. He couldn't knock at the door. Then he finally did.

Pinocchio waited and waited. Finally a window on the top floor opened. Pinocchio saw a big Snail with a lit candle on her head looking out of the window. "Who is there at this time of night?" she asked.

"Is the Fairy at home? It's me, Pinocchio," he said.

"The Fairy is sleeping and can't be awakened. Who is Pinocchio?" the Snail asked.

"I am the puppet who lived in the Fairy's house," he answered.

"Oh, yes!" she said. "Wait for me there. I'll come down and open the door."

"Be quick. I'm freezing!" Pinocchio said, sighing.

"My dear boy, I am a Snail and am never in a hurry," the snail replied.

Pinocchio waited at the door for hours. At last he knocked again and this time he knocked louder than before. A window on the lower story opened, and the same snail with the candle on her head appeared.

"I have been waiting here for hours. Please hurry!" Pinocchio whined.

A few hours later, the door was still closed. Losing all patience, Pinocchio kicked the door. It was such a hard blow that his foot went through the wood and got stuck.

At daybreak, the door opened at last. The little Snail had taken nine hours to come down from the fourth floor of the house to the door.

"Why is your foot stuck in the door?" she asked, laughing.

"It was an accident," Pinocchio said. "Can you try to free me from this trap?"

"My boy, we'll need a carpenter for that job," the Snail said. "I have never been a carpenter."

"Please get the Fairy for me!" the puppet begged.

"The Fairy is asleep and must not be disturbed," the Snail replied.

"At least bring me something to eat. I'm starving," Pinocchio said.

"I will, at once," the snail said.

Three hours later, the Snail returned and said, "The Fairy sent you this breakfast."

Pinocchio was very pleased to see this delicious feast. But when he began to eat he was quite annoyed to discover that the bread was made of plaster, the chicken was really cardboard, and the apricots were glass!

Pinocchio wanted to cry. He tried to throw away the tray but he was so upset and tired that he fainted.

When he woke up, he was lying on a couch and the Fairy was standing beside him.

"I will forgive you one more time, Pinocchio," the Fairy said sternly, "but don't misbehave a third time! I will not be so quick to forgive you again!"

Pinocchio promised that he would study and that he would always be good and obey her from then on. For the rest of the year, Pinocchio kept his word and was on his very best behavior. He didn't even miss one day of school!

The Fairy was very pleased. "Tomorrow your wish will be granted,"

she said one day, smiling at him kindly. "Tomorrow you will no longer be a puppet. You will become a boy."

Pinocchio was thrilled. To celebrate the special event, the Fairy told Pinocchio that she would prepare a wonderful breakfast feast. It was going to be a delightful day and Pinocchio jumped and danced with joy. But, in the life of a puppet, there is always something that ruins everything.

CHAPTER 19
Funville

The Fairy gave Pinocchio permission to go around town and to give out the invitations for the special breakfast.

"I promise to be back in an hour," the puppet said.

"Be good, Pinocchio," the Fairy said.

"Why should I?" Pinocchio asked.

"Because boys who don't listen to the advice of those who know better always end up in trouble," she said.

"I know that," Pinocchio said. "I'll never make that mistake again."

"We'll see," the Fairy said.

In less than an hour all of his friends

were invited to the breakfast. All but one, that is. His name was Candlewick because he was so thin and tall. Candlewick was the most lazy and most naughty boy in school. Pinocchio was especially fond of him. After going to his house three times, Pinocchio found Candlewick waiting for a coach.

"Where are you going?" the puppet asked.

"I am going to Funville," Candlewick said. "Why don't you come with me? It's the best place for boys. There are no schoolteachers and no books. No one there ever studies. Every day is a day off. And holidays begin on the first day of January and end on the last day of December. Doesn't it sound great?"

"I don't know," Pinocchio said. He shook his head. The idea sounded good to him, but he wasn't sure.

"Will you go with me?" Candlewick asked. "Hurry up and make up your mind."

"No, I can't. I promised the Fairy I'd be

good and I'll keep my word. I must return home at once. Have a good journey, Candlewick," Pinocchio said.

Pinocchio took two steps, stopped, and then turned back.

He asked, "Are you really certain that every day is a day off?"

"I am certain," Candlewick said.

"You're sure that all holidays begin on January first and end on the last day of December?" Pinocchio asked.

"I am sure," Candlewick said.

"What a great place Funville is!" Pinocchio said with a dazed look on his face. "I mean...good-bye! Have a very pleasant journey," Pinocchio muttered.

"Bye," Candlewick replied, "I'll be going soon."

Nighttime had come and it was already very dark. In the distance, Pinocchio and Candlewick could see a small light moving. They heard talking noises and the faint sound of a trumpet.

"It's here!" Candlewick shouted.

"What is it?" Pinocchio asked.

"It's the coach to Funville. Now will you come, Pinocchio?" Candlewick

asked.

"Is it really true," Pinocchio asked, "that boys never have to study in Funville?"

"That's right. Never!" Candlewick said.

"What a wonderful place!" Pinocchio said with glee.

The coach was drawn by twelve pairs of donkeys. Each donkey was a different color. But the oddest thing about these donkeys was that they all wore men's shoes.

The coachman was a flabby little man with a small, round face. He was always laughing. All of the boys loved the coachman as soon as they saw him. They all wanted to get in his coach and go to Funville.

The coach was full of boys between eight and twelve years old. They were all piled on top of one another. No one cared. They were so happy to be going to a land that had no school teachers and no books that they just went on their way without a care in the world.

When the coach reached Candlewick, he jumped on board. But Pinocchio still wasn't sure if he wanted to go.

"I'll stay here," Pinocchio said. "I am going to study and learn like good boys do."

"Pinocchio!" Candlewick called out. "We'll have so much fun!"

Pinocchio sighed. "Make a little room for me. I'm coming, too!" he finally said.

Pinocchio had to sit on one of the donkeys. So he went to the first pair and tried to climb up onto one. But the donkey kicked Pinocchio over. All the boys began to laugh.

The coachman approached the unruly beast. He pretended to kiss him, but he actually bit off half of his ear. Then he said, "You can climb on now without fear. I've had a little talk with our donkey friend. I'm sure he's gentle as a lamb now."

Pinocchio mounted the donkey, and the coach started moving. While the donkeys galloped and the coach rattled over the stones, Pinocchio thought he heard a whispering voice. "You always follow your own way. Well, you'll be sorry for it!" it seemed to say. Pinocchio looked from side to side to see where the voice was coming from. There was no one there.

They arrived at Funville at dawn. The population was made up only of boys. Everyone was having a wonderful time. There were all kinds of merry noises and shouting as groups of boys played everywhere.

Pinocchio, Candlewick, and the other boys who had just arrived in the coach had barely set foot in town before they were totally caught up in its activities.

Where could you find more content boys?

For five months, Pinocchio enjoyed a carefree life in Funville. Every day was filled with fun and amusement. Every time he saw Candlewick, he thanked him for bringing him there. The days were spent doing nothing but playing. No thoughts of schoolteachers or books ever entered Pinocchio's wooden head. But one day something happened that upset him very much.

CHAPTER 20

Pinocchio Becomes a Real Donkey

When Pinocchio woke up and scratched his head, he discovered he had grown ears—donkey ears! He began to cry. The more he cried, the longer his ears grew.

At the sound of his cries, a Squirrel that lived on the first floor came into Pinocchio's room. "What has happened?" she asked.

"I am very sick," the puppet said.

"You have donkey fever!" said the Squirrel.

"In a little while you won't be a puppet or a boy," she said calmly. "You will be a donkey."

"Oh, no! How awful!" Pinocchio cried.

"Poor Pinocchio," the Squirrel said. "There is nothing you can do now. All boys who are lazy and who hate schoolteachers and books and spend all their time having fun sooner or later end up turning into little donkeys."

"Is that really true?" Pinocchio asked, sobbing.

"Yes it is. You should have known," the squirrel said.

"I am a puppet with no sense and no heart," Pinocchio said, sighing. He went out to find Candlewick, whom he blamed for this entire adventure.

Pinocchio went to Candlewick's house and knocked on the door. "Who is there?" Candlewick asked.

"It's me," Pinocchio said.

"Just a moment and I will let you in," Candlewick answered.

Thirty minutes later, the door opened and Pinocchio saw that his friend was also suffering from donkey fever!

Instead of feeling miserable, they began to flick their ears and laugh. Then Candlewick suddenly stopped laughing. He staggered and said, "Help, help, Pinocchio!"

"What is wrong?" Pinocchio asked.

"I can't stand upright anymore," Candlewick said.

"Neither can I," Pinocchio said as he began to cry.

They both doubled over and began to run around the room on their hands and feet. As they ran, their hands became hooves and their faces changed into donkey muzzles. They became covered with gray hair. How humiliated they felt when they grew tails!

"Hee-haw, hee-haw," was all they could say.

Then someone knocked at the door. "Open the door! It's the coachman who brought you here. Open the door, or you will be sorry!" he yelled.

CHAPTER 21
Sold to the Circus

The coachman kicked down the door and entered the room. "Good for you," he said with his usual laugh. "You boys bray very well."

The two little donkeys stood with their heads down, their ears lowered, and their tails between their legs. The coachman was going to take them to the market to sell them to the highest bidder. He was a wicked man who took all the lazy boys to Funville. They turned into dumb donkeys that he could sell for a handsome profit. He'd become a very rich man doing this.

"Let's go," he said heartlessly, taking them to the market.

That very day Candlewick was bought by a peasant. Pinocchio was sold to the ringmaster of a circus, where he would learn to perform with the other animals. From that day on, Pinocchio had to endure a very hard life.

When Pinocchio complained about having to eat hay or straw, the man would punish him. After this, Pinocchio didn't complain anymore.

Poor Pinocchio had to learn to jump through hoops, dance, and stand on his hind legs. It took him a few months to master all of this. During that time, he was constantly whipped.

Finally the day came when Pinocchio was brought before the crowd.

After the first portion of the circus performance, the ringmaster—dressed in a black coat with white tights and big leather boots—came into the center ring and presented Pinocchio. The audience applauded. He had a new leather bridle with shiny buckles and studs, and a white flower in each ear. His mane was curled and tied with bows. He was wearing a gold and silver belt around his body, and his tail was braided with velvet ribbons.

Then the ringmaster took a deep bow and turned to Pinocchio, saying, "Courage, Pinocchio! Before you begin your tricks, bow to the audience—ladies and gentlemen and children..."

Pinocchio obeyed and bent both his

knees till they touched the ground. He remained kneeling until the ringmaster, cracking his whip, shouted to him, "Walk!"

After a little time, the ringmaster said, "Trot! Canter! Full gallop!" Each time, Pinocchio obeyed the order and changed his gait.

But while he was galloping full speed, the master raised his arm and fired off a pistol. At the shot of the gun, the little donkey pretended to be wounded and fell to the ground.

As he got up there was an outburst of applause. He raised his head to look up. In one of the boxes he noticed a beautiful lady who wore a thick gold chain with a medallion that had a portrait of a puppet painted on it.

"That's me! That lady is the Fairy!" Pinocchio said to himself. He tried to cry out, "Oh, my Fairy!" but instead of those words, "Hee-haw, hee-haw" was all he could say. It was so loud that all the people watching the show laughed, especially the children.

To teach him a lesson not to bray in public, the ringmaster hit him on his nose with the handle of the whip. Poor Pinocchio licked his nose to try to ease the pain. When he looked up again, the Fairy was gone!

Pinocchio's eyes filled with tears, and he began to sob. No one noticed, not even the ringmaster, who cracked his whip again and shouted, "Courage, Pinocchio! Let the audience see how gracefully you can jump through the hoops."

Pinocchio tried, but his right leg got caught in the hoop and he fell. When he got up he was lame.

The next day, the animals' doctor came to see Pinocchio and said that he would be lame for the rest of his life. The mean ringmaster sent the stable boy to sell the lame donkey at the market.

"How much do you want for that lame donkey?" a man asked.

"Twenty dollars," the stable boy said.

"I'll give you two dollars. I only want his skin so I can make a drum with it for my town band," the man said.

The buyer paid his two dollars and took the little donkey to the seashore. Then he put a stone around its neck, tied a rope around its leg, and pushed the donkey into the water.

Weighed down by the heavy stone, Pinocchio sunk right to the bottom.

CHAPTER 22

In the Belly of
the Shark

An hour later, the man began to pull on the rope that he had tied to the donkey's leg. He pulled and pulled until. . . he couldn't believe his eyes! Instead of a dead donkey there was a live puppet.

"What happened to the donkey that I threw into the sea?" he asked.

"I am the little donkey!" Pinocchio said, laughing.

"But how can this be? Just moments ago you were a little donkey. How could you become a wooden puppet?" the man asked.

"Untie me and I'll tell you," Pinocchio said.

The man was curious and untied the rope.

When Pinocchio was free, he told the man the entire tale of how he went to Funville and became a donkey that was sold to a circus, became lame, and ended up being sold to be made into a drum.

"Is that the end of your story?" the man asked.

"No," Pinocchio answered. "It was the good Fairy who saved me."

"And who is this Fairy?" he asked.

"She is my mama and she is like all other good mothers who care for their children and who never lose sight of them, helping them no matter what. The good Fairy saw that I was drowning and she sent a school of fish to eat the dead donkey's skin. What mouthfuls they took!" Pinocchio said.

"From this moment on," the man said, "I'll never touch fish again. It would be too awful to open one and then find a donkey's tail inside!" The man told Pinocchio that he was going to sell him.

"Sell me if you want to," Pinocchio said as he jumped into the water and swam away from the shore. "Good-bye, master. If you ever need a donkey skin to make a drum, think of me." Pinocchio laughed.

While he swam, Pinocchio thought he saw a pretty little Goat, standing on a rock in the middle of the sea, calling out to him. The little Goat's hair was blue. It was the same color blue as the hair of the beautiful little girl.

Pinocchio swam twice as hard to reach the rock. When he was halfway there, he saw the horrible head of a sea monster coming up out of the water toward him. The monster's wide mouth was open and was as big as a cave. It was the gigantic shark that had been seen the day that old Geppetto was lost at sea.

Pinocchio was terrified at the

sight of this monster and tried to change the direction of his swimming.

"Hurry, Pinocchio, hurry!" the little, blue Goat called.

Pinocchio swam as fast as his arms and feet could carry him.

"Hurry, Pinocchio, hurry! The shark is right behind you!" the Goat yelled.

Pinocchio had almost reached the rock and the little Goat reached out to help him, but it was too late! The huge monster overtook him. With a deep breath, the shark sucked in poor Pinocchio. The sea monster swallowed him and Pinocchio fell, unconscious,

into the shark's stomach.

When he woke up, Pinocchio couldn't understand where he was. It was very dark. At first he tried to keep up his courage. But when he realized that he was really in the body of a sea monster, he began to cry and scream and sob. "Help me! How unfortunate I am. Will no one save me?" he cried.

"Who do you expect to save you?" asked a Tuna that had been swallowed by the shark at the same time.

"What are we going to do now?" Pinocchio asked.

"Wait to be digested," the Tuna said.

"I don't want to be digested," Pinocchio responded.

"Me either," the Tuna said, "but being born a fish, I know it's better than to end up in a frying pan."

"That may be your opinion, but I want to get out of here," Pinocchio cried.

"Escape if you can," the Tuna said.

"Is this shark very big?" the puppet

asked.

"Big! His body is two miles long without his tail!" the fish exclaimed.

While they were talking, Pinocchio saw a light. "What is that?" he asked.

"Probably someone like us waiting to be digested," the Tuna said.

"I'm going to find him. Maybe he can show us how to escape," Pinocchio said.

Pinocchio left the Tuna and walked in the direction of the light. When at last he reached it, he saw a man seated at a table with a candle in a bottle. The man was Geppetto!

"Oh, my dear papa!" Pinocchio shouted. "I have found you finally! I will never leave you again—never, never, never!"

"Are my eyes tricking me?" the little old man asked. "Is it really you, my dear little Pinocchio?"

"Yes. It's really me! Have you forgiven me? Oh, my dear Papa, how good you are to forgive me," Pinocchio said.

"How long have you been in here?" the

puppet asked his father.

"For many days," Geppetto said.

"How did you survive?" the puppet asked.

"Another ship was swallowed in the same storm that overturned my boat," Geppetto said. "The sailors were all saved, but the ship went to the bottom. The shark swallowed the ship and then he swallowed me."

"How?" Pinocchio asked.

"He swallowed it in one mouthful. I was lucky that the ship was full of preserved meats, and boxes of matches. But I'm just about to run out of everything. This candle is the last one," Geppetto said.

"Then there is no time to waste," Pinocchio said. "We must think of a way to escape."

"How?" Geppetto asked.

"Through the shark's mouth and then into the sea, where we'll swim to shore," Pinocchio said.

"But I don't know how to swim," Geppetto said.

"I'll carry you," Pinocchio said.

They walked for a long time, traveling through the body of the shark. When they arrived at the point where the shark's big throat began, they stopped to look around and to choose the best moment to escape.

"Now," he whispered to Geppetto. "The shark is sleeping. We'll be safe soon!"

With Geppetto on his shoulders, Pinocchio jumped into the water and began to swim.

Pinocchio Becomes
a Boy at Last

"Have courage, Papa! We are almost on shore," Pinocchio said, knowing his father was growing weak. But Pinocchio was tired, too. He was out of breath and didn't think he would make it to the shore. But they finally did.

Pinocchio offered his arm to Geppetto to help him stand. "Lean on me, Papa. We'll walk very slowly and find a place to rest," he said.

They hadn't gone far when they saw two people begging. They were the Fox and the Cat, but they were hardly recognizable. The Cat, who for so long had pretended to be blind, was really blind now. The Fox was old and he was paralyzed on one side of his body, and his tail was gone. He had to sell it to buy food.

"Oh, Pinocchio!" the Fox cried. "Can you give a little something to two poor people?"

"Poor people," the Cat repeated.

"Get away, you imposters!" Pinocchio cried. "You tricked me once, but you'll never do it again."

Pinocchio and Geppetto went on their way and soon saw a straw house in the middle of the fields. They went

in and looked all around but could see no one. "Where is the master of the house?" Pinocchio asked.

"I am up here," a voice replied.

Geppetto and Pinocchio looked up at the ceiling and saw the Talking Cricket.

"I will take pity on both of you. But, remember, in this world, whenever it is possible, we should help others if we wish to be given help in our hour of need," the Cricket said.

"You are right, Cricket. I will always remember that lesson. How did you get this house?" Pinocchio asked.

"A goat whose wool was a beautiful blue color gave it to me yesterday," the Cricket said.

"Where is the goat now? Will it come back?" Pinocchio asked.

"No. It went far away, grieving and muttering something about poor Pinocchio being swallowed by the shark," the Cricket explained.

"Then it was my dear little Fairy!"

Pinocchio exclaimed.

Pinocchio set up a bed for Geppetto. "Where can I get a glass of milk for my papa?" he asked.

"There's a farm not far from here. The gardener will help you," the Cricket said.

Pinocchio ran all the way to the gardener's house and asked for a glass of milk.

"It costs a one coin. Give me the money first," the gardener said.

"I don't have any money," Pinocchio said.

"Can you work at a water-pumping machine?" the gardener asked.

Pinocchio said he would try. The nice gardener took him to the machine, where he worked for the afternoon.

For five months Pinocchio worked at the pumping machine every day to earn a glass of milk to help Geppetto get well. He also learned to make baskets and earned money selling them. He was able to take care of all of his and Geppetto's expenses. He even managed to save some money to buy a new coat for Geppetto.

One day when he left the house, he heard someone calling him.

"Don't you know me? I was the maid to the Fairy with the blue hair," a Snail said, crawling out from under a bush.

"I remember!" Pinocchio shouted. "Where is my good Fairy?"

The Snail replied, "She has been overwhelmed by problems and is so ill,

she can't even buy food."

"Oh, poor Fairy! I have only two gold coins. Take the money. I was going to buy a new coat, but take it to my good Fairy," Pinocchio said.

That night, Pinocchio dreamed that he saw the beautiful good Fairy. She kissed him and then said, "Well done, Pinocchio! You are forgiven for all that's in the past. You have a good heart. Boys who take care of their parents deserve great praise and affection, even if they can't always obey. Try and do better always and you will be happy."

Pinocchio's dream ended, and he opened his eyes.

Imagine how surprised he was when he discovered that he was no longer a wooden puppet. He had become a real boy, like all the others. He glanced around and saw that the walls of the hut had disappeared and that he was in a nice room with new furniture. He jumped out of bed and found a new suit and boots. In the pocket of his jacket he found fifty gold coins and a note from the Fairy thanking him for his most kind generosity.

He finished dressing and went into the next room. Geppetto was there and was well again. He was already working at his trade, woodcarving a beautiful frame.

"Tell me, Papa," Pinocchio said, as he hugged and kissed Geppetto, "how can this change have happened?"

"It is all your doing, Pinocchio," Geppetto said to his son. "Because when boys who have been bad turn over a new leaf and become good, they have the

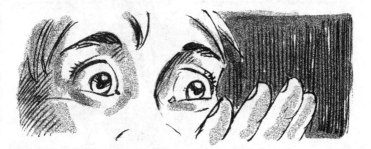

power to bring such happiness to their families."

Pinocchio saw the old wooden puppet in the corner. He gazed at it a while and finally said, "How silly I was when I was a puppet! How glad I am now that I have become a nice little boy!"

About the Author

Carlo Lorenzini, better known as Carlo Collodi, was born in Florence, Italy in 1826. Collodi is a small town outside of Florence where he was raised.

Collodi developed two loves in his years of schooling–writing and music.

At the age of twenty, Collodi began to write music reviews for an Italian magazine, and later began working as a government official for the Education Department in Italy.

In 1876, Collodi decided to devote himself to writing for children because he felt that adults were too hard to please. His first children's book, Giannettino, was a huge success.

In 1881, Collodi wrote a story about a naughty wooden puppet's search to become a boy. In 1883, The Adventures of Pinocchio was published as a book. Within years, the book became a classic with both children and adult readers.

Carlo Collodi died in Florence, Italy in 1890.

The Adventures of Tom Sawyer
The Adventures of Pinocchio
Alice in Wonderland
Anne of Green Gables
Beauty and the Beast
Black Beauty
The Call of the Wild
A Christmas Carol
Frankenstein
Great Expectations
Journey to the Center of the Earth
The Jungle Book
King Arthur and the Knights of the Round Table
Little Women
Moby Dick
The Night Before Christmas and Other Holiday Tales
Oliver Twist
Peter Pan
The Prince and the Pauper
Pygmalion
The Secret Garden
The Time Machine
Treasure Island
White Fang
The Wind in the Willows
The Wizard of Oz